CHARGING INTO FATE

Also by Alexandria Blaelock

SHORT STORY COLLECTIONS
The Histories of Hayward Hall
Lovelorn, Lovestruck and Love at First Sight
Common or Garden Variety Heroes
Case Files of the Wilkinson Detective Agency
Unavoidable Fates
Christmas Travesties
Five Faces of Felicia Clarke
Little Place Called Home
Security Directorate Dossiers v. 1.
Security Directorate Dossiers v. 2.

FICTION
That Love Nonsense
Taipan vs Brown
The Ghost and Ms Cox
Friends Like That
Weaving the Wildwood
Wolf vs Orb

MS BLAELOCK'S BOOKS
Stress Free Dinner Parties
Signature Wardrobe Planning
Holistic Personal Finance
Minimally Viable Housekeeping
Planning a Life Worth Living

PICTURE BOOKS
Australia Felix

SELECTED SHORT STORIES
Alma's Grace
Blood and Bloody Profanity
Cancelled by the Cartel
Dingo Hunting
Honoris Virilis Respectu
Mince Pie Mystery
Remains of Christmas

CHARGING INTO FATE

A FATES SHORT STORY

ALEXANDRIA BLAELOCK

BlueMere Books

MELBOURNE, AUSTRALIA

For permission requests, please contact enquiries@bluemerebooks.com.

Ordering Information:
Discounts are available on quantity purchases. For details, contact orders@bluemerebooks.com.

Charging into Fate/Alexandria Blaelock
paperback ISBN: 978-1-923083-12-7
digital ISBN: 978-1-923083-13-4

Book Layout © BookDesignTemplates.com
Cover Art © Warm_Tail licenced from Shutterstock.com

CHARGING INTO FATE

Last bookshop 1,000 km." Marguerite read the sign aloud as it flashed past.

"That's funny isn't it? That should really read last servo."

"Hmmm?" said Steve.

"Last bookshop."

"Yeah, right," he mustered up a chuckle though she could see his mind wasn't really on it.

She sighed and looked out the window again.

Miles and miles of flat, black, bushfire scarred land; scrub bushes regrowing low on the ground with the odd burnt out tree trunk standing like a dark statue from a long-ago civilisation.

As they flashed past another trunk, she thought it looked like a man fallen to his knees with his hands thrown up.

She whispered, "My name is Ozymandias, King of Kings," out the window, quoting Percy Bysshe Shelley.

Not spoken out loud, because she knew Steve was not a big fan of poetry.

He thought she was being uppity, flaunting her middle-class upbringing before him. Showing off.

She watched Ozymandias recede into the distance with the side mirror and corrected herself.

Miles and miles *and* miles of burnt-out bush.

It made her heart ache, though she couldn't say what for.

The creatures that once lived there?

The extent of the devastation?

Or that it reminded her of her own life.

Trashed and burned, an empty wasteland of neglected and forgotten dreams. And she was fairly sure it was all because of Steve.

Well, not all Steve, obviously she had a hand in it too.

But somewhere along the line, she'd forgotten who she was.

And a crap tonne of show-offy poetry.

She knew Steve was planning to dump her. And given he'd blown through all her savings; it was only a matter of time.

Weeks if not days.

He probably had a new mark, primed and ready to go.

She knew exactly how it would happen.

One day he'd just move in with the next girl and disappear, leaving her to deal with the fallout; probably superannuation funds stripped bare, loans and credit cards she didn't know she'd taken out, and overly aggressive debt collectors.

But that was okay.

The day after that, she'd start picking up the pieces, and she'd be glad.

Marguerite vowed she would never allow herself to blindly trust someone like that again.

Weird though that he wanted one last holiday. A trip along the Coral Coast; Perth, Geraldton, Shark Bay, Carnarvon, Exmouth.

Staying at the Cape Range National Park, to look at the gorges and the reef, and then coming home

Aside from being with Steve 24/7, she was having a good time.

Idly she wondered what the last bookshop would be like.

She imagined something like an old wood cabin, half falling down, the boards scoured clean of paint by the strong coastal winds.

Perhaps there was a single petrol bowser out the front, one of those old manual ones that had dinged as the thingy turned in a globe so you could see and hear the petrol pumping.

And they'd have a café, half full of junk with a table or two, selling dry, old pies a week or two old.

More likely it would be someone's idea of a joke - no one read books any more.

They'd do better selling handicrafts. Allegedly made by natives like they did in America.

Steve slowed the car as he approached a fork in the road.

In the middle of the fork sat a roadhouse.

An oddly charming, more or less modern, red brick construction with a well-maintained parking lot and a grassy area with gas barbecues and pic-nic settings.

It was fascinatingly at odds with the burnt-out bush surrounding it, and she wanted to go in and check it out, but Steve drove right by it, as if it didn't exist.

If nothing else, she'd have welcomed a decent shower given they'd been camping for a few days without running water.

She opened her mouth to ask to go back, but as she turned towards him, she saw his jaw tense and decided not.

He'd just ruin it for her anyway.

Maybe on the way back.

After all, they might know a bit more about the Last Bookshop.

Steve drove right through to the village, and then a little further to a parking lot almost on the beach.

Marguerite got out of the car and stretched. The burned-out bush gave way to a stretch of white sandy beach and blue green sea, with actual fish in it, took her breath away.

Absolutely stunning.

She clawed her long hair back from her face, and swept it back up into a pony tail. Freeing her sweaty neck to catch the drying seaweed scented breeze off the ocean.

And a sprinkling of beach sand as well.

Steve was the beachy one of the pair, while she preferred the bush. But aside from the sun-burn she was getting, she was glad to be there; somewhere away from the ordinary.

Something about the sun coming at her from all directions was refreshing and invigorating, rather than being shaded by office blocks as she was all day at work.

Or under the shifting shadows of the trees in her garden at home.

Someone nearby laughed, for a moment louder than the seagulls begging for hot chips.

You'd think they'd be bored of chips, wanting something different for a change.

"Go get some cold drinks and I'll see if there's a room at the hotel," he said.

She nodded and wandered down the street, looking in the windows for drinks.

Next to no time later, someone grabbed her arm firmly; her head whipped round, saw it was Steve carrying the look of thunder.

Reflexively, she looked at her watch to see if she'd taken too long.

"Stupid hotel has no rooms. We have to back up down the highway, somewhere called the Palace Hotel."

"Oh, we passed it on the way in."

"Did we? I didn't see it."

Marguerite couldn't imagine how he'd missed it given its size, but he was clearly irritated, so she didn't say anything.

Now wasn't the time to be getting "uppity" as he called it.

She took the safe way out and grunted; he could interpret that anyway that took his fancy.

"Let's go," he said, and started dragging her back up the street.

By the arm.

Not transferring his grip to her hand.

"You don't want to see what's here before we leave?" she asked, a little bit sulkily because they had after all just arrived.

"Nah, it's late. Let's go."

Marguerite wanted to look at her watch again, because she was pretty sure it wasn't that late.

Though the evenings seemed to stretch out like full days themselves, and the night fell suddenly.

But she meekly followed him back to the car.

It wasn't worth getting into an argument about that.

Steve had no trouble finding the Palace Hotel this time.

He barely slowed at the entrance and arrived in the central parking lot with a squeal of tires.

He slammed the car door, and stamped his way up the stairs and into the hotel.

With more time to look at it, she could see two arms running down each leg of the Y.

One with petrol bowsers, and the other a small hotel complex; its faded sign reading Palace Hotel.

A café in the centre, with a small general and souvenir store with an enclosed outdoor.

Through elaborate ironwork gates, she could see an enclosed outdoor eating area with a sign declaring it dog-friendly.

Marguerite stopped to pat the ageing Labrador sunning itself on the verandah.

As she waked inside, she was surprised to see a kind of mid-century modern reception area. A sort of glassed-in sun room, conservatory thing with terrazzo floors.

A young red-headed woman standing at the polished red wood reception desk was smiling politely and just starting her spiel.

"Welcome to the Palace Hotel, my name's Diana. How can I help you today?"

"Room please," Steve snapped.

Marguerite could see he'd about reached his limit, and crossed her fingers that poor Diana would speed up and get the conversation over and done with before he exploded.

She sat on the edge of a nearby slim, wood framed chair, preparing herself to intervene if necessary.

The dog from the verandah wandered inside and sat beside her, putting his head in her lap.

She looked down at it and started scratching his head. It cocked his head to give her better access behind its ears.

She wasn't sure exactly what happened next, but suddenly Diana was kneeling before her saying, "excuse me, are you okay?"

She jumped and sat bolt upright, which startled the dog enough to stand up and back away a few paces, then she craned her neck looking left and right for Steve.

"It's okay, I sent him to the bar with a free coupon."

"Oh. I... The room. I."

Diana smiled, and rested a hand on Marguerite's arm, "are you okay?"

"I." She took a deep breath and tried again, "I'm fine, thanks for asking."

Diana looked at Marguerite's lap where her fingers were tightly woven together.

"I'm not sure that's entirely true, is it?"

Marguerite looked into Diana's soft brown eyes and went as still as a rabbit caught in head-lights.

"He hasn't treated you well, has he?"

Marguerite didn't say a word.

"Your Spidey senses are telling you something's not quite right, aren't they?"

Even if she could've broken eye contact with Diana, Marguerite couldn't have said anything.

Even if she'd wanted to.

Diana tucked a fallen lock of hair behind Marguerite's ear to better see her face, and said "it's not safe for you here with him, is it?"

Marguerite managed to swallow and look away.

"Wouldn't you like to visit the bookshop?"

After a long pause, in which Diana said nothing, Marguerite spoke as of she was in a dream. "I would actually. I meant to ask you about that."

She snapped back into the room, "wait. What do you mean I'm not safe?"

Diana sat back on her heels, "there's just something about a hunter only another hunter can see."

Marguerite looked at the dog, and it looked back at her.

It was true.

She'd been walking on eggshells since they'd left, trying not to upset him.

Trying not to give him an excuse.

An excuse to...

She *really* wasn't safe.

But.

She didn't know what to do about it.

And she didn't think she had the strength to do anything, even if she knew what the best thing to actually do was.

"Why don't you visit the bookshop? I'm sure that will help clear your mind."

"I couldn't possibly drive Steve's car without his permission."

"So? Take mine."

"I really couldn't."

"You really could."

Diana got up, revealing her feet were bare, and walked behind the reception counter, coming back with a set of keys she threw at Marguerite, "it's the red Valiant Charger in the parking lot."

Marguerite caught the keys, then twisted her body to look into the lot, and then back at the woman.

"That's *your* muscle car?"

She put her hands on her hips, seemingly amused by Marguerite's reaction, "sure is."

"But you seem..." she blushed and dropped her head.

Diana laughed, "looks can be deceiving."

Marguerite grinned, "if you loan me that car I might never come back."

"Don't worry about the car, she *always* finds her way back."

Marguerite weighed the keys in her hand.

Aware that Steve wouldn't be happy when he found out she'd gone out on her own.

Getting in Diana's car and driving away would change her one way or another.

"Won't the shop be shut by now?"

"I can give them a call and ask them to wait for you."

She looked at the keys; old and worn as they were.

On the cusp of a seemingly small and insignificant decision, she felt as though the universe was holding its breath to see what she might do.

She looked up at Diana's knowing gaze, seeing something older and wiser than the woman appeared to be.

"Yes. Okay then, yes.

"I'll visit the bookshop."

"Perfect," Diana said, "turn left as you leave the hotel - it's closer than you think. Just let them know I sent you."

Marguerite walked out the door, got in the car and turned the key before she could change her mind.

And before Steve could catch her.

The car roared into life with a loud enough rumble of thunder to call the dead back to life.

Certainly loud enough to startle a flock of cockatoos into life, squawking their dismay as they launched from the trees into the air.

Marguerite slowly backed out of the parking bay, feeling as though the car wanted to drive more than she did.

Turning left, letting it rip, and rocketing up the highway.

But you can't cruise without tunes, so she turned the radio on and randomly pushed a button to tune it.

The sound of Jet blasted from the concealed speakers, "Bring it on Back", if she remembered correctly. One of her favourites.

It was on the jukebox when she'd first met Steve.

Thirty seconds earlier, or thirty seconds later and she'd have missed him.

Gone for that other guy, what was his name?

The cute one.

So appropriate for the situation she found herself in at that moment.

She belted out the song.

And then, suddenly, the bookshop leapt into being on the highway as she approached it.

Or at least it was probably the bookshop though it looked more like a house.

She pulled in, parked a little way from both the road and the shop, and turned off the engine.

With the throbbing engine silenced, it was so quiet she was convinced she could hear electricity crackling in the air.

The shop was almost exactly as she imagined it.

An old weatherboard building, the sun setting behind it, possibly held together by dead termite nests, its white paint peeling to reveal weathered grey boards.

No petrol bowsers, and no café.

Three women sat on Adirondack chairs arranged in a curve under an awning stretching out from the roof. They shared a round table, on which sat a wine bottle and four glasses, three of them half full.

The woman closest to her was twenty-ish, wearing tight red jeans and t-shirt. A strawberry blonde plait hung down one shoulder.

She was sitting cross legged, and appeared to be knitting, but what was dropping from her nee-dles was more like a tangled ball of different threads than something coherent like a beanie or maybe a cardigan.

The woman in the middle looked fortyish, and sprawled in her seat, legs and feet akimbo. She was wearing a black skirt and open-collared shirt, fanning herself with a black fan.

Her black hair was caught up on her head with something like a chopstick, exposing the back of her neck to what passed as a cool breeze.

There was an empty chair between her and an ageless woman with short white hair, and a long white dress.

She sat upright, one leg slung across the other, gently swaying in time to a tune Marguerite could almost hear.

She held a pair of scissors in her hand, and was using one blade to trim splinters from the table.

Marguerite shook herself and got out of the car.

Not exactly sure what to expect, though the scene before her made her think more of an out-door wine bar than a bookshop.

All they needed was a fire pit to make it more like a beach barbecue.

She walked towards the women, "Um. Hi. Diana sent me?"

"Would you care to join us for some wine?" the white-haired woman asked.

Marguerite found herself wanting a glass of wine more than anything else in the world. "That would be lovely if you have one to spare."

The black-haired woman patted the empty seat beside her. Marguerite sat down, allowed the blonde to pour her a glass of Rosé.

"Cheers," she said, raising her glass to the women, who raised theirs and they drank together.

"Oh, that's lovely," Marguerite said, her face brightening, "it makes me think of one Summer when I was about fifteen and the carnival came to town. I fell madly in love with a handsome brown eyed boy who worked the dodgem cars."

She smiled fondly as she looked back.

"How could I have forgotten about him? What was his name?" She looked up into the sky trying to remember.

"Something exotic. I can picture him now, and on my god, he was so beautiful. I went back every day for the week to see him."

The blonde smiled at her, "how did it turn out?"

Marguerite's face fell. "Ah. He moved away when the carnival closed, and I never saw him again. But before he left, he gave me my first kiss - he was such a good kisser."

Marguerite smiled for a moment at the memory, and then looked at the blonde woman, "I sometimes wonder what happened to him, and who he married, and whether he's happy."

"Ah, your first love. What do you think happened?" the black-haired woman asked, and Marguerite laughed.

"I'd like to think he still pines for me even now, but I actually hope that wherever he is, he's happy. With a job he loves, a wife he adores, and a life that makes him happy."

She took another sip of her wine as the black- and white-haired women looked at each other. The black raised an eyebrow, and the white shook her head a little.

Marguerite took another sip of wine, and said, "it's funny how life turns out, isn't it?"

"Yes," the dark-haired woman replied.

"Goodness," said Marguerite, "how rude of me! My name's Marguerite."

The women went round the circle, saying their names.

"Claudia," said the blond.

"Laura," the black-haired woman.

"Agatha," the white-haired.

"I'm very pleased to meet you," said Marguerite.

And she really was, but couldn't have said why. Maybe because she was just relaxing as the wine took effect.

"And what's your current boyfriend like?" asked Laura, "is he nice? Does he make your heart race like your first love?"

"Chalk and cheese," Marguerite drained the glass, "to be honest, I think he's going to dump me."

She looked into her empty glass, and Claudia filled it up again.

"But I don't care; I wish he was dead," she drank some more.

"Actually no, I don't wish he was dead. And I don't really wish I'd never met him. He was so sweet in the beginning. I..." she waved her hands around, sloshing a little of the wine from the glass and over her hands.

She put the glass down and licked it from her hands and fingers.

"You what?" asked Agatha.

"I wish I hadn't been naive enough, or maybe foolish enough to get in so deep so quickly. That when he tried to move in, I'd said no. That when he asked for money, I'd said no. That I was a stronger person. Less desperate for love."

"Wish you'd met the boy at the carnival again?" asked Laura.

"Maybe. When your first is so blissful, I think it sets you up to be a loser in love forever."

"I expect that's all the fairy tales we hear when we're children," said Claudia.

"So cynical for one so young," said Agatha,

"Do you think there's one true love for everyone then?" asked Laura.

"I used to," Marguerite reached for the glass, and Claudia filled it up again. "Now I think love is more of a love for right now thing. Maybe you're lucky and you grow at the same pace, but more likely one of you changes more than the other and you break apart."

"Some people never change," said Agatha, "some people never grow up or move on."

"Like Steve. He's like a perpetual child, and when he uses up one woman, he discards them and moves onto the next."

"Are you sure he moves on," asked Claudia, "have you ever met any of his past girlfriends?"

"Ummmmmm. No, I don't think I have," Marguerite yawned widely, extending her neck to put her face in the air.

"And did you ask him why he wanted to take a trip with you right now?" asked Laura.

Marguerite rested her elbow on the table, and leaned her head on it. "Um, no. I thought it was just a last goodbye. Why do you ask?" she yawned again.

"Did you consider that maybe he doesn't plan to break up with you? Maybe he wants to kill you?" asked Agatha.

"That's very dark..." Marguerite mumbled, "why on earth would you ask that?"

She started snoring.

The following morning, she woke alone with a slight hangover which she put down to drinking without eating.

And the remains of a dream about three women and a bookshop. Who'd changed her life somehow.

She took a long hot shower, washing the grease of several days camping from her body and her hair.

As she looked in the mirror to comb her hair, something was bugging her, but her head hurt, and she was so agitated she couldn't quite put her finger on it.

She took some clean clothes out of the drawer, fairly sure she hadn't unpacked, and all her clothes needed washing.

There was no sign of Steve, his bag hadn't been touched, but the car was not in the lot where he'd left it.

For a moment she panicked, thinking he'd abandoned her, then remembered his bag hadn't been disturbed.

Besides, when she was looking at the route, she recalled seeing reference to a coach line.

If the worse came to the worst, there was always a bus.

Even with the car, there was no point looking for him, no doubt he'd turn up. Annoyed about something or another.

At the café she ordered a strong latte and sat on the verandah to drink it.

It was still Summer, but the morning air had a chill in it, so she dragged a chair into the morning sun.

She couldn't be bothered going back to the room for something warmer, so while her back warmed up, she still shivered a little with the cold in her front.

The hotel dog wandered by, then came back and sat leaning on her leg, sniffing up at her as she bent to scratch its head.

She saw a police car driving up the highway, and as she watched it turned in and parked.

After a moment, a tall dark-haired guy got out. He put his hat on, she guessed to signal that this visit was for business, and started walking towards the hotel.

The dog fidgeted, and he turned his head towards her as he walked. Registering her presence, he touched his hat and she nodded in acknowledgement as he walked up the steps and into the hotel.

A short while later, Diana brought him outside and introduced him to her, "Marguerite, this is Senior Sargent Victor Moreno, and he—."

The Police Officer put his hand on Diana's arm to stop her saying anything further.

"I'm making enquiries about the last known movements of," he took a notebook from his breast pocket, flipped it open and after consulting is, "Gerald McEvoy."

Marguerite gaped at him.

"I don't know any Gerald McEvoy!"

"Yet you checked in with him yesterday evening."

"I checked in with Steve Lewis."

He glanced at Diana, wrote something in his notebook, then asked Marguerite, "what is the nature of your relationship with this Steve Lewis?"

"He's my boyfriend."

"And have you been dating long?"

"Only feels that way."

He raised an eyebrow at her, "I don't know, couple of months? Six months tops."

"And where were you last night?"

"She was in the bar 'til late," Diana said.

He frowned at her.

"I'm just saying. She was very drunk, and probably doesn't remember. We took her back to her room at about 2 am."

He rubbed his eyebrows, "your license to serve alcohol expires at midnight."

"As you well know, we stop serving alcohol at midnight. But being a Roadhouse, the premises are open 24 hours a day for food and other beverages."

He sighed, "let's see the tape then."

Curious, Marguerite tagged along.

They all crowded into the manager's office, even the dog.

Diana sat at the desk and queued the playback on her laptop. They watched the replay, a little clock in the top left-hand corner running through the time.

It started just before she and Steve walked in. Her recollection of the evening was quite different, but she didn't say anything.

Diana paused the playback to show Steve leaving at about eight, and he made a note in his book.

Marguerite was fascinated by the footage of her eating and drinking, talking to people she didn't recognise, and then falling asleep at the table.

And after a while, Diana and another woman picked her up and took her out.

Diana slid the mouse and queued footage of the car park. Steve walked out, got in the car, and drove off. The playback continued as Diana explained, "the room was empty when we got her into it, and the bed hadn't been slept in."

A few trucks came and went, but right up until that moment, there was no sign of Steve.

"So what's this about?" Marguerite asked.

"I regret to inform you that the body of Gerald McEvoy, or as you know him, Steven Lewis was discovered this morning."

Marguerite sat down, but with no chair to catch her, she fell to the floor.

Unable to get a grip on her emotions.

Unsure whether to laugh or cry.

Fully aware that Senior Sargent Victor Moreno was there to witness everything.

She felt bad for wishing him dead.

Because despite what Diana's video had shown, she knew she'd driven off in her red charger to find the bookshop.

Skipping out on Steve, and not worrying about him in the slightest.

"I think she's gone into shock," Diana told the Senior Sargent, "perhaps it would be best if you came back later?"

He seemed reluctant to leave, but eventually nodded and left.

Diana helped her up.

"I wished he was dead."

"Wishes don't create reality. Come and get another coffee."

Marguerite looked at her.

She shrugged and pulled Marguerite through to the café, "not that kind of reality anyway.

"According to Moreno, hikers found his remains some way off the highway. They think he was attacked by wild dogs."

"But when I was at the bookshop, I wished he was dead. What if they say something?"

Diana went behind the espresso machine and started making two coffees, "they won't say anything to the Police because the bookshop is the kind of place that only appears when someone needs it."

"And you said wishes don't change reality."

"Maybe it wasn't your wish? Did you consider that?"

Marguerite gave her a blank look.

Diana hesitated, and something in Marguerite's made up her mind, "maybe all the other women he brought here finally got their re-venge."

"What do you mean all the other women?"

Diana smiled grimly and handed her a coffee.

After sipping her own she said, "you're not the only one he's brought through here. One every few months for the last few years."

Marguerite's face paled, "how did he explain that?"

"Sisters, cousins, girlfriends."

"What do you think happened then?"

"I think in a few days, they're going to start digging up dead women."

And that was exactly as much cold hard reality as Marguerite could deal with at that moment.

"I think I need to go back to bed and wake up this morning again."

"Sleep well."

Back in her room, fully made up despite the early hour and the mess she'd left behind, she curled up on her side and pulled the bedspread over herself.

There had to be more going on here than met the eye.

Three women running a bookshop that was only there when you needed it. Claudia... Clotho? Knitting something that looked messed up and tangled. Like her life if she was honest.

"Diana" running a hotel.

Steve torn apart by wild dogs.

Yes, she'd wished him dead, and suddenly, maybe magically, she was free of him.

And then she remembered the thing that was bugging her, and went back to the bathroom to check it.

She had a hazy memory of cutting her hair at the bookshop, and sure enough it was several inches shorter.

And she hadn't over-soaped it, like you normally do when you cut your hair. Nor had Diana mentioned it to her.

But the dog had seemed to know something was different about her.

What bargain exactly had she struck for her hair? She had to find out.

She walked over to the charger, and she looked around to see if anyone was watching before opening the door. The keys were still in the igni-tion, and shortly after that, she was turning left and zooming along the highway.

An hour later, she was approaching the next town and still hadn't seen the bookshop.

She was tempted to keep going, but was sure she hadn't made it this far the day before.

In any case, she didn't really *need* the bookshop. Assuming she had before.

Shouldn't they have given her a contract?

No, that was deals with the devil.

Regretfully, she turned the car around and headed back.

She hadn't even got a book!

Diana was leaning on a verandah post when she got back.

"You're not going to tell me?"

"I don't know the details. They are a law unto themselves; even I'm not immune to their powers, so I don't ever push them."

"But what did they do?"

"All I can tell you is that now and again I do them a favour, and then again and now, I just steer someone who needs them their way."

"Like maybe you go hunting?"

She let the silence grow.

And then she pulled a book from behind her back and held it out, "they asked me to give you this."

Marguerite took the book and walked past Diana, taking the book and walking through to the bar.

"Vodka tonic," she told the barman. When the drink was ready, she paid and took it to a seat in the window.

She plunked the book face down on the table, arranged so all she could see were the edges of the pages. The old pages. And the beautifully tooled, possibly leather cover.

What, she wondered, was she supposed to tell the Police Officer when he came back.

For that matter, what was she supposed to do with the rest of her life?

She took a sip of her drink, then dragged the book towards her, turned it over and opened the cover.

The front page was empty.

She turned the page, and that was empty too.

Picking it up, she flicked through all the pages, and they were all empty.

Marguerite turned back to the front, and flipped the first page again. As she looked, a picture emerged from the page.

It looked like a party photo of grinning women, but more like the kind of painting you see as a frontispiece in an old book.

She was about to slam the cover shut, but the woman brandishing a fist full of hair caught her eye; it was her. With Claudia, Laura and Agatha surrounding her.

And then some faded, spidery handwriting came into focus on what would otherwise be the title page.

Your fate is unwritten,

Here's to making your own destiny.

Suddenly starving, she flagged a waitress down for a menu, and a few moments later, ordered a country meat pie with vegetables and mash.

Someone stood next to the table, "may I join you?" Senior Sargent Victor Moreno asked.

She shrugged.

He sat opposite her, took his hat off and sat it on the chair between them.

"This is a bit off-topic, but I feel like I've met you before."

"I don't think so. I'm not sure I've ever met anyone called Victor Moreno."

"Ah, my parents died in an accident when I was young and I went to live with my aunt and uncle. When they adopted me, they changed my name so I wouldn't always be reminded of them."

"Oh, that's... sweet. I guess.

"I don't come from here; I grew up in rural Victoria.

"My parents were carnies, and they travelled a rural circuit through Victoria?"

Marguerite thought about her conversation with at the bookshop. "Traralgon?"

"Wait," he fumbled for his wallet, and pulled a set of photo booth picture out, old and worn where generations of wallets had creased them.

"You have to be kidding me," said Margeurite.

"No, really. Is this you?"

And of course he was the boy from the summer carnival.

If you'd got as far as a bookshop that wasn't there, and a book waiting to be written, who else could he possibly be.

Though she had to admit to herself, if not to him, that she was happy to meet him again.

Though she wondered, just a little bit, whether he'd always been there, or they'd pulled him from somewhere else for her.

"To be honest," he said, "this puts me in a bit of a bind."

"Yes?"

"Well, I came to tell you not to leave the area until our enquiries have finished, but there was something about your silhouette in the window."

"I see. You want to get to know me, but you can't until you've cleared me as a suspect. Presumably until the case is closed."

"Ah, yeah. Though it just got complicated. You see, we found human remains in the bush near where Gerald McEvoy parked his car."

"So, it might take some time," she struggled to repress a smile.

"Yes."

"Well, I have a couple of weeks leave from work, and it seems I don't have any plans as such..."

"Oh, well that's great. I mean fortunate. For the investigation."

She sipped her drink, "indeed it is."

THE END

As a small token of my thanks for reading...

Please enjoy 10% off everything (excluding shipping)

at alexandriablaelock.com

with the code margueriteten.

Turn the page for some ideas where to use it,

The Histories of Hayward Hall

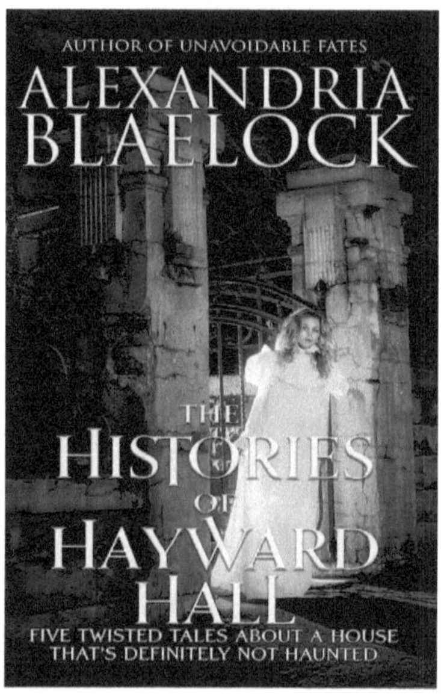

Meet Morag Clementine. The new housekeeper at historic Hayward Hall.

Her practical and capable attitude usually keeps her out of trouble.

bove all, her no-nonsense, get it done approach. And her get in the middle of the scrum outlook. Just as well, because Hayward Hall needs someone like her.

In this genre-spanning collection of original stories, Morag finds herself ensnared in the History of Hayward Hall...

No ordinary housekeeper, can Morag save the house, one century at a time?

Common or Garden Variety Heroes

Do you have what it takes to be a hero?

Whether that's running into a burning building, standing up for what you know is right, or saving the Princess it's going to take everything you've got and more besides.

In this genre-spanning collection of original stories, five women draw on resources they didn't know they had.

Join them, if you dare.

Perhaps you'll carry your new books in one of these bags

And enjoy them while you're drinking
from one of these mugs

ABOUT THE AUTHOR

Australian author Alexandria Blaelock writes mostly fantasy and mystery.

She's appeared in the Stringybark Anthology *Crowd Surfing*, *Pulphouse Fiction Magazine*, and *Ellery Queen's Mystery Magazine*.

She's also written five self-help books applying business techniques to personal matters like getting dressed, tidying up, and feeding friends.

When not exploring parallel universes, she talks to animals, indulges in K-dramas, and sips Campari. She lives in the Dandenongs, where she relishes the sound of birdsong, the scent of gum leaves and the sun on her face.

Discover more at https://alexandriablaelock.com.